The Sleepover Club

Have you been
invited to all these
Sleepovers?

Sleepover on Friday 13th

by Louis Catt

Collins
An imprint of HarperCollinsPublishers

The Sleepover Club ® is a registered trademark
of HarperCollins*Publishers* Ltd

First published in Great Britain by Collins in 1998
Collins is an imprint of HarperCollins*Publishers* Ltd
77-85 Fulham Palace Road, Hammersmith,
London, W6 8JB

1 3 5 7 9 8 6 4 2

Text copyright © Louis Catt 1998

Original series characters,
plotting and settings © Rose Impey 1997

ISBN 0 00 675392 2

The author asserts the moral right to be
identified as the author of the work.

Printed and bound in Great Britain by
Caledonian International Book Manufacturing Ltd,
Glasgow G64

Sleepover Kit List

1. Sleeping bag

2. Pillow

3. Pyjamas or a nightdress

4. Slippers

5. Toothbrush, toothpaste, soap etc

6. Towel

7. Teddy

8. A creepy story

9. Ghoulish food for a midnight feast

10. A torch

11. Hairbrush

12. Hair things like a bobble or hairband, if you need them

13. Clean knickers and socks

14. Sleepover diary and membership card

CHAPTER ONE

It's odd, isn't it? I mean, Thursday the 7th, or Monday the 24th – I bet you never even notice those days! Well, not unless it's your birthday or something like that. I mean, have you ever forgotten your own birthday? No! Of course not – and I'd never forget mine – it's June 9th, the best ever time of year to have a birthday because it's exactly half way between Christmas.

And I'd never forget the birthdays of the rest of the Sleepover Club either. Not that they'd let me! Just imagine if I forgot Frankie's birthday! She's my best mate, but she'd still kill me if I forgot. Actually, I suppose I'd kill *her* if she forgot *my* birthday – but I bet we'd make up soon after. Frankie and I are like that – we're always arguing, but it doesn't mean anything. Frankie says we argue because I'm a Gemini and I can't ever make up my mind (which isn't true). I say it's because she's an Aries and she's a pig-headed ram. Well, maybe she isn't exactly pig-headed – but she does like to boss us about...

Lyndz has four brothers so it always seems to be someone's birthday in her house. Her mum makes just the coolest birthday cakes! She used to be a domestic science teacher, and she's a whizz at cooking. When Lyndz's little brother, Ben, was four her mum made him a chocolate cake in the shape of a gorilla, and it was the scrummiest thing you've ever eaten. Lyndz's birthday is in October. Frankie says she's a typical Libran – easy going and always trying to keep the peace. She even seems to like her brothers.

I don't know how I'd feel about four brothers. Lyndz says it's OK, so maybe it is. I've got two older sisters, Emma and Molly. And believe you me, two sisters is the worst thing that could ever happen to anybody, especially when one of them is like my sister Molly.

Nobody has got a sister as awful as she is – I call her Molly the Monster, and I think that's being really nice. The worst thing is we have to share a bedroom, and she fusses and moans non-stop. I can't leave one sock on her side without her going *mad*. And what's really unfair is she won't even let me keep my rat in the room! I tell her it's cruelty to animals, but she doesn't listen. She just puts on this stupid face and says, "Oh Laura, I do wish you'd grow up!" She knows I hate it when anyone calls me that. The rest of the Sleepover Club call me Kenny, because of my surname – McKenzie.

Fliss has her birthday soon after the summer holidays and she starts planning her cake the second term starts... not to mention all her presents! One year she had a cake covered with little pink roses and purple ribbons. Frankie said she just *knew* Fliss would be wearing purple ribbons in her hair – and she was! All the presents from Fliss's mum were tied up with pink and purple string – and you can guess what colour the balloons were! Fliss's mum must have spent ages and ages getting everything to match… but she's like that. I think Fliss is, too. Maybe it's because she's a Virgo. Frankie says Virgos like everything to be perfect.

Rosie's the fifth member of the Sleepover Club. Her birthday's July 15th. The last one after mine. Rosie's mum makes a huge thing about her birthday. I think it's because she worries that Rosie doesn't get as much attention as her brother and sister, so she makes it up to her then. Frankie and I were talking about it the other day, and we both think Rosie deserves a special birthday.

But hang on, I'm sidetracking. Why was I talking about birthdays? Oh yes! I was saying that mostly people don't notice what day and date it is... but Friday 13th. *Eeeeeek*! You always notice *that* date. And that's the day we had this *totally* scary sleepover at my house. I'll tell you all about it in just a minute... it was brilliant.

I don't know if you're superstitious. I'm not, not really – but Friday 13th *does* make you feel a bit creepy, doesn't it? And if you drop a cup, or fall over, or break something, you can't help thinking it all happened because it's an unlucky day, even if you fall over twice as much on other days.

It's also a great day for telling horror stories and, as you know, I *love* horror stories. I know some true ones, too, because my dad's a doctor, and sometimes he tells us stories about what happened in the old days. Did you know that doctors used to saw off people's legs while they were still wide awake? It's true. They'd give them a bit of leather to chew on, but that's all. And when they were finished they just threw the old leg into a bucket – and by the end of the day the bucket was full of legs!

Does that give you chills up and down your spine? It did when Dad told me – but I'm going to be a doctor when I grow up, so I've got to get used to all that kind of stuff. I practise by watching TV programmes like *Casualty* – and even when there's blood everywhere, I love it!

I told the Sleepover Club about the bucket full of legs and Frankie said it was the best story she'd heard in ages. Fliss said it was disgusting – she's a bit squeamish about things like that – but she still went and told her younger brother. And then her mum told me off because he woke up in the night screaming.

I think it might have been the leg story that started Frankie and me thinking about Friday 13th. Frankie had the idea to have a sleepover on that night, but it was my idea to make it a really really special one… well, I'm sure you'll agree, it was much too good an opportunity to miss. We were going to make sure we had the creepiest, scariest

Friday 13th ever!

Lyndz and Rosie thought it was a brilliant idea. Only Fliss didn't, which wasn't a great surprise. She said she couldn't come because she goes to tea with her dad and his new baby on Fridays.

Frankie stared at her. "But you're always home by about half-past six," she said.

Fliss wriggled, and went pink. "I might have to stay later," she said.

Frankie shook her head. "Felicity Sidebotham," she said, "are you scared?"

Fliss went even pinker. "Of course I'm not," she said, but her voice was a little bit wobbly.

Lyndz patted her arm. "It'll be OK," she said. "We'll just have a lot of fun."

"Yes," Frankie said. "Lots of *scary* fun!"

"I'm not scared!" Fliss said, but she still sounded squeakier than usual.

"So does that mean you'll come?" I asked.

"Of course I will," she said. "Just as long as you don't go too far."

That made me laugh. I told Fliss she

sounded just like her mum. Fliss tossed her head and said she didn't, but we all knew that that was exactly what her mum would have said. Looking back on it now, maybe we should have taken more notice... but of course, we didn't!

CHAPTER TWO

Everyone came round to my house after school the next day so we could sort out a plan. A Friday 13th *super* plan! We grabbed a packet of choccy biscuits, some crisps and a coke each, and sneaked up to my room. Molly the Monster was out somewhere, so we piled up the pillows and duvets from her bed and mine and made ourselves really comfortable.

"We need to make a list," Frankie said. "Where's a pen?"

I found a stubby old pencil under my bed. It's always exciting, looking under my bed.

The weirdest things pop out sometimes, and I know I haven't put them there.

I mean, there was the time when Emma lost her best trainers. Anyone would have thought she'd lost the crown jewels, the way she went on about it. She kept looking at me, too, and she knows I don't have the same size feet as her. Well, not quite. I have to stuff loads of extra socks on if I want to wear Em's shoes.

Anyway, even Dad got involved and he ordered a *huge* search. And guess where they were? Yes – that's right. Under my bed! I told Dad they must have walked there by themselves, but he just made a sort of *humph*! noise.

The problem was, in the hunt Mum found Molly's homework diary under my bed, and Monster Features said it was *my* fault! Can you believe it? I never touched her diary, and if I'd known it was there I would've given it back to her. I don't want *anything* of Molly's in my half of the room.

Then Dad went on about the other

things... two pairs of jeans (dirty), one sweatshirt (crumpled), one bag of rat food (just a little bit open), last week's maths test (scrumpled), half a bar of chocolate (melted), lots of bits of paper, an empty coke can, one clean blue sock, one smelly green sock, one bedroom slipper, three pens, an old rubber... and some very interesting fluffy bits.

Mum had a go at me, too, and Molly moaned and groaned. It went on for ages. Personally I don't know what they were fussing about.

But there I go, sidetracking again. I was telling you about our sleepover, wasn't I? So, anyway, I found the pencil and tore a piece of paper out of an old notebook. Then we got planning. Frankie wrote down:

1. Check sleepover OK with Kenny's mum.
2. Get rid of Molly.

I sighed when she put down number two. Some chance! If Molly has a friend to stay I'm quite happy to make myself scarce and share Emma's room. There's always loads of interesting things to poke around in in there, so you'd think Molly would be pleased to do the same for me... but oh, no. She hates moving out of our room, and she hates all my friends, too.

"Maybe she'll be away that night," Fliss said hopefully.

I began to giggle. "Yeah – after all, it *is* Friday 13th! Maybe she'll be off scaring small children!"

"Frightening little old ladies!" said Lyndz.

Rosie sniggered. "Turning the milk sour on people's doorsteps!"

"Sending murderers screaming home to their grannies!" Frankie shrieked.

That cracked us all up. We rolled about on the floor, we were laughing so much. Some coke cans fell over and the crisps got scrunched into the carpet, but we just couldn't stop.

At last we sat up, and I scrabbled around for the piece of paper. It had got very soggy, so I tore out another sheet and we started again.

"What shall we do about food!" I yelled.

We all started grinning at each other. As you know, food is a favourite Sleepover Club subject.

"Green spaghetti!" said Frankie.

"Green pizza!" said Lyndz.

"Green jelly spiders!" shrieked Rosie.

"Green jelly worms!" said Fliss with a shudder.

Frankie looked excited. "Maybe we could make a huge bowl of green slime! We could put the jelly spiders and worms in it – and then everyone has to eat them without using fingers!"

"Yeah!" I said. "Cool!"

We've only just discovered green slime. Actually, it was Lyndz who invented it. Rosie was round at her house and they were helping Lyndz's mum make green jelly. Lyndz was supposed to be stirring the jelly cubes in hot water to make them melt, but she was talking to Rosie and didn't stir them enough. Then she put in just a bit too much cold water by mistake.

"Whoops!" Lyndz said. "Oh well. I don't suppose it'll matter," and she tipped the whole lot into the bowl where it was meant to set... but it never did! It turned out all slithery and – well, slimy. The bits of jelly cube that hadn't quite melted were floating on the top. When Lyndz and Rosie fished them out and ate them they were like jelly sweets – all rubbery. Ben, Lyndz's little brother, thought it tasted gross, but Lyndz didn't, and neither did Rosie. They ate the whole lot... with straws! We've been eating green slime ever since. It's a Sleepover Club special!

"What else?" Lyndz asked. "What other food is creepy?"

I was playing with the pencil. "Um... I don't know."

"OK." Frankie snatched the pencil off me and turned to face us all. "So what sort of things shall we do? How can we set it up so it's really scary?" She wrote *Plans*! on the paper, and drew a creepy face with long pointy teeth underneath.

Fliss gave a little shiver. "We don't want to go too far…"

We all started eyeballing each other and Fliss quickly shut up.

"Booby traps!" I said. "We ought to have booby traps! And horrible noises!"

Frankie let out a loud and horrible wail. She was sitting right next to me with chocolate crumbs all over her face… but still it sent a quivery chill up my spine. Fliss squeaked, and Rosie and Lyndz clutched each other.

"Wow!" I said. "Maybe we could tape you! That'd sound completely gruesome in the dark—"

I didn't get a chance to finish. Frankie gave another wail and grabbed me. "Kenny. You're a genius! That's it. We'll make the spookiest tape ever, full of shriekings and wailings!"

"And horrible gurglings!" shouted Rosie.

"Slow dragging footsteps!" yelled Lyndz.

Even Fliss was beginning to look enthusiastic.

We were so excited we didn't hear the banging. We were all jumping up and down on my bed, and I was waving a pillow round and round – just as Molly burst through the door. It wasn't my fault she walked straight into the pillow.

"*Oooof!*" Molly made an amazing spluttering noise and sat down on the bed with a flump. She looked so funny we all fell about laughing.

It was a pity Mum was right behind her. We had really and truly meant to tidy up all the crisps and crumbs – and of course we were going to make the beds. It's always the same though, I expect you've noticed – no one ever surprises you when your room is all neat and tidy and spotlessly clean. No, it's only ever when it's totally upside down. And upside down was exactly what my half of the room was – and Molly's half wasn't much better.

We got it sorted out. Well, we had to. Mum stood in the doorway with her arms folded until it was back to normal. Molly tried to boss us about, too, but luckily the phone went and Mum sent her downstairs to answer it and she was gone ages.

I didn't ask Mum about having a sleepover straight away. It didn't seem quite the right moment. Just then she seemed really keen on getting rid of everybody – not on having them around. Still, I wasn't too worried, I was sure I could find a way round her somehow, even if it meant doing the washing-up or some other gruesome task for a week. It was going to be the best sleepover ever – and nothing was going to stand in our way – we just had to make sure Molly didn't stick her nose in and spoil it!

CHAPTER THREE

After the gang had gone I went back inside expecting to find Molly waiting to yell and scream and throw a fit or two – all in my direction. I was ready for it – but it never happened! She was in the kitchen talking to Mum, and as I went past she actually waved at me – if you'd been there you would have heard my jaw fall *thunk* on the floor. I leant against the wall to recover. Yes, OK I leant against the wall to recover *and* to see if I could listen in and find out what was going on. Wouldn't you have done the same?

"That's fine," I heard Mum say. "It'll be

nice for you to have a night away with a friend, and it's not as if you have school the next day. You can collect your things when you get home from school, and I'll give you your bus fare then."

My jaw thunked on the floor for the second time in minutes. Molly going away? With a friend? And then it clicked... Mum had said she wouldn't have any school the next day – Molly was going to be away on Friday night!

It took a ginormous effort not to dash to the phone that second and ring Frankie and Fliss and Lyndz and Rosie. But somehow I restrained myself. Somehow I managed to stay where I was until Mum and Molly had finished chatting, and Molly was back on the phone.

"Zoe?" she said. "Mum says it's OK. I'll zoom home from school and get my stuff, and then I'll catch the first bus over."

As soon as Molly was out of the way I wandered into the kitchen trying to look as if I didn't really want anything. Mum was tidying up, so I thought it might be a good idea to hang up a few mugs. After all, it wasn't *that* long since I'd been blasted for being messy, untidy, and a few other things that I couldn't remember.

Mum looked at me suspiciously. "Hmm," she said. "Let me guess… you want to have a sleepover here on Friday night." Then she nodded. "I don't see why not. It'll be much easier for you with Molly away – but I want your room spotless by the time she comes back again!"

I gave her a huge hug. "I promise!" I said, and I meant it. Cross my heart and hope to die. Then I helped put away all the rest of the crockery.

I had to wait until school the next day to tell the others. Mum said the phone bill was already staggering under the weight of all my calls, and I'd only said goodbye to my friends half an hour before. When I burst into the cloakroom and told them that the sleepover was all fixed *and* Molly was going to be away Frankie whooped, Lyndz cheered and Rosie grinned all over her face. Only Fliss shuffled a bit.

"What's the matter?" I asked. "You're not chickening out after all, are you?"

Frankie banged Fliss on the back. "You said you'd come!"

Lyndz nodded. "It wouldn't be the same without you," she said.

Fliss started to look really pleased. For a moment I felt bad, and I wondered if we were a bit hard on Fliss sometimes.

Then she shuffled her feet again. "It's the burglar," she said. "My mum isn't sure if I should spend the night away from home."

We all stared at her. "Burglar?" Rosie said. "What burglar?"

"It was in *The Mercury*," Fliss said. "Three houses were broken into last week, and another one this week. One of the houses was just round the corner from where I live!"

Frankie gave a loud snort. "You'll be just as safe at Kenny's house as you are at home," she said. "After all, it's only a burglar

– it's not a murderer."

Fliss went even pinker. "My mum says it might not be safe. She says burglars often murder people if they get in their way."

Frankie made another snorting noise, but Lyndz patted Fliss's arm. "We could come and collect you," she said. "I could ask my mum to drive us both to Kenny's house."

Fliss looked a lot happier. "That would be great," she said.

I wasn't really taking much notice. *I* was thinking that things were getting better by the minute. Friday 13th – no Molly – a spooky sleepover – and now a burglar on the loose! What more could we ask for?

"Hey!" I said. "Maybe we could hunt down the burglar and catch him! Is there a reward, Fliss?"

Lyndz gave me a push. "Shut up!" she hissed, because Fliss was staring at me in her rabbit-caught-in-the-headlights kind of way. Catching burglars was about the last thing she would think of as fun.

"Just kidding," I said, but I didn't look at

Frankie. I was pretty sure that she was thinking the same as me. But we didn't have time to discuss the sleepover any more, because the bell for registration rang.

At lunchtime we got into a huddle to talk about the food, and Fliss was a lot more cheerful. She said she'd make a green cake, and when Rosie said she hoped it would be green inside, as well as having green icing, Fliss giggled and said, "Of course it will."

I wondered if Fliss would have green hair ribbons to match.

"Bags I make the green spaghetti," Rosie said. "I'll put currants in it, and they'll look like dead flies."

"Or spiders without legs!" said Fliss, and we all laughed.

Lyndz said she'd already had an idea for a scary pizza. "What?" Frankie asked, but Lyndz shook her head and wouldn't say. She's completely brilliant at cooking so we didn't make her tell us. If she had a good idea it was worth waiting for!

"I don't mind doing the green slime and the jelly spiders and worms," I said. "But what are you going to do, Frankie?"

Frankie rolled her eyes. "Wait and see!" she said. "Slugs and snails and puppy dog's tails!"

"Yuck!" said Fliss, but she didn't look totally grossed out.

You know I said how my jaw kept falling open so I looked like a gasping goldfish? Well, it happened again. As I staggered in through our front door that afternoon, I met Emma coming out with some girl I didn't know.

"Hi," I said, although I didn't expect a reply. Sometimes Emma pretends I'm invisible when she's with someone. Either that, or she talks to me as if I'm about six and she's my ageing aunt. Today I was lucky, this time it was the ageing aunt.

"Hi," she said, and ruffled my hair. She knows I hate it, but she still goes on doing it. "Look, Jade – this is my kid sister, Laura."

Jade gave me the sort of look you'd give a passing beetle. "Oh," she said.

"She's got loads of funny little friends," Emma said. "They have a club, and they all sleep over at each other's houses. Cute, isn't it?"

Jade didn't look as if she agreed, but she nodded anyway. "Yeah. Cute."

Emma ruffled my hair again. "You can really have fun on Friday, little sister," she said. "I'm going to stay with Jade for the weekend. And she and the strange girl walked off.

I stood and stared after them, my jaw doing its thunking thing. Emma was going away for the *whole weekend*. Wow! And an idea crept into my head, and once it was there it grew and grew and grew: if I put all Molly's things in Emma's room, I could clear my room right out! For the first time ever we could have loads and loads of space!

I could just imagine it. No Molly hanging around telling us not to touch her things. No squeezing three extra sleeping bags onto the tiny bit of floor between my bed and Molly's. I could push Molly's bed right against the wall, push the dressing table back… or we could move the beds the other way… I dashed to the phone to tell Frankie, and to ask her to come round as early as she could on Friday to help.

Frankie was just as pleased as I was. Then she said something that I'd been thinking. I'd been *thinking* it, but not saying it on purpose. I suppose I was being superstitious – you can't be too careful around Friday 13th, can you? But then Frankie came right out and said it.

"It all seems too good to be true," she said. "Isn't Friday 13th meant to be an unlucky day?"

So I'm blaming all the things that happened after that on Frankie.

CHAPTER FOUR

I woke up really early on Friday 13th. Molly was still fast asleep with her mouth wide open. *Gross*! I thought about seeing if I could flip something in, but I decided not to. After all, she was going to be away for the night of our sleepover. Maybe if I was nice to her she'd go away again...

I decided to start fixing up some of the booby traps and tricks ready for the evening. Frankie was coming home with me after school to make our scary tape and to help move the bedroom furniture... but I thought there was no harm in getting started. And anyway, I had to plan something special for Frankie! I slid out of bed and tiptoed out of the room.

Down in the kitchen I had a good look round. I knew exactly what I wanted to do – I wanted to arrange something so that Frankie had a fright. Yes, I know she's my very best mate – but she wouldn't be angry with me, she'd just think it was really funny. Besides, I had a sneaky feeling that she might have a plan or two up her sleeve for me, too.

I stared at the cupboards, hoping for inspiration. It didn't help much, so I opened a few doors and peered in. Flour? Could be useful. Sticky syrup? Maybe. I opened a jar of raisins, and ate some. Looking at them made me giggle – they looked just like mouse droppings! A few in the corner of my room might be fun… Fliss might be fooled for a minute or two! But what could I do that Frankie wouldn't expect? She was bound to be suspicious of drawers and cupboards in my room… I needed a much more cunning idea! I ate a few more raisins and climbed on a stool to look in the top cupboard... and then it happened.

Whoooooosh!

I nearly died of fright. Something soft and dusty and furry flew straight at me. I fell off the stool with a crash. My heart was pounding and my knees had turned to jelly as I stared wildly... at my old hot-water bottle!

OK, OK, I know. hot-water bottles are pink and rubbery. But remember when you were little and relatives gave you furry, cat-cover hot-water bottles, and brown, teddy hot-water bottles, and cosy clown hot-water bottles? One Christmas I had *four*! Talk about boring. And I hate hot-water bottles anyway – I'm always worried they might burst and splurge boiling water all over me while I'm asleep.

So Mum had put them away. And obviously this was one of them. I picked it up. It was a furry black cat, but it was totally covered in dust – it must have been in the top cupboard for ages and ages. Then, while I was looking at it, a ginormous light bulb switched itself on in my head. This was it! This could be my special surprise for Frankie! After all, it had scared *me* silly; I was still feeling fluttery inside. As it had done that to me – wouldn't it do just the same to Frankie? Yes! I said to myself. *Yes! Yes! Yes!*

I was about to put the cat back exactly how it had been, when I had another thought. I grabbed the bag of flour and gave it a thorough dusting… just for that little extra effect. Then I climbed back on the stool. I could see why the cat had sprung out the way it did. The cupboard was so small I had to bend the hot-water bottle to fit it in, which made a natural spring! I grinned happily as I wiped my hands and put the flour back on the shelf.

"Laura? Don't tell me you've got up early just to make your old dad a cup of tea!"

I jumped in a guilty sort of way, but Dad didn't notice. He was looking his usual morning self – all crumpled, and half-asleep.

I didn't want to make him suspicious, so I put the kettle on without making a fuss, while he got out the teapot and cups. Then I made us both some toast, fetched the paper and we sat down to breakfast together.

"This is a very pleasant surprise," Dad said, and he yawned. "It'll set me up for a terrible day. I've got surgery, then house calls, and then this evening I've got to go to a meeting… and I'm introducing the speaker so I've got to dash back here and get all dressed up in my suit."

"Poor old Dad," I said, and I meant it. He works really hard and is always having to dash around all over the place. It's a tough life being a doctor – but that hasn't put me off!

"Look at this!" Dad said suddenly. He was reading the paper. "There's been *another* burglary! In just the next street. Well, they'd better not try getting in here. There's nothing for them to take, but it won't hurt to be careful."

"I'll make sure all the doors and windows

are shut before I leave," I said. "And I'll tell Mum to be extra careful, too."

After I'd finished my toast I went to get ready for school. Molly looked very surprised when she saw I was up before her, but she didn't make any nasty remarks. I decided it must be because she had a friend. Wow, I thought. This is actually turning out to be a Really Good Day!

All through assembly I kept thinking of how I'd jumped when that dusty old cat flew out at me. It made me smile, and Frankie started to give me sideways looks.

"What was so funny?" she asked when we all met up at first break.

"Nothing," I said. "I was just thinking about tonight."

Lyndz gave a little whoop. "Just wait till you see my pizza!" she said. "Tom helped me – we had a totally ace idea!"

"My spaghetti's turned out a bit odd," Rosie said. "We didn't have any green food colouring so I thought I could mix blue and yellow, but it hasn't really worked."

"You should have phoned me," Fliss said. "My mum bought two kinds of green for my cake."

Frankie nudged at me. Trust Fliss.

Fliss saw the nudge, and pulled a face at us. "My mum says if a thing's worth doing, it's worth doing well. Anyway, you haven't told us what you're bringing yet, Frankie?"

"Ah! Wait and see. It's a surprise," Frankie said.

"I didn't see you carrying anything to school," Fliss said. "And aren't you going straight home with Kenny?"

"Congratulations!" Frankie banged Fliss on the back. "I proclaim you... Felicity Sidebotham, Junior Detective!"

"I was only wondering," Fliss said, sounding all huffy.

"Well, you'll just have to keep guessing," Frankie said. "Nothing will be revealed until tonight... the night of Friday 13th!" And she made a ghoulish face.

Rosie squeaked, and we all laughed – Fliss

too. Then the bell went, and we had to go back into lessons.

That afternoon, on the way back from school, I looked at Frankie's school bag slung on her back – Fliss was right, it didn't look as if there was anything much in it at all.

"Have you really made something for tonight?" I asked.

"Wait and see!" Frankie said, and I knew it wouldn't be any good asking her any more about it. She's brilliant at keeping secrets. I wouldn't find out about this one until she was ready!

CHAPTER FIVE

Emma wasn't there, of course, when Frankie and I crashed in through the front door. She was already safely on her way to her friend Jade's house. Molly was still at home, though. She growled at us when we charged into our bedroom.

"Can't you two kiddies go and play somewhere else? I'm *trying* to get my things packed!"

Honestly. You could tell Molly hadn't stayed the night with anyone for years. She had two sets of pyjamas on the bed, three pairs of socks and four different T-shirts –

she looked as if she was going away for weeks! I could have told her all she needed was a toothbrush and something to sleep in, but I didn't. I pulled Frankie out of the room and we went down to the kitchen. It looked cleaner and tidier than usual; the floor was positively gleaming! A note from Mum lay on the table:

CAKE IN TIN. DON'T MAKE A MESS –
NEW NEIGHBOUR COMING IN FOR TEA.

"Ace!" Frankie said. "I love your mum's cakes." She went to the tin and got the cake out while I found us some coke.

"We might as well eat down here," I said. "With any luck Molly will be gone soon – and then we can really get busy. I haven't made the slime jelly yet."

"OK." Frankie cut two huge slices of Mum's cake. It was chocolate – and one of her very best. The icing was thick and gooey, and the cake was soft and squidgey. Awesome!

We were cutting ourselves a second piece when the doorbell rang.

Frankie jumped up. "That might be for me!" she said, and we both raced for the door.

Frankie's mum was standing outside, and she was holding two big cardboard boxes.

Frankie let out a loud whoop and rushed towards her. "Mum! You're a star!"

"I know." Frankie's mum smiled, and handed one box to Frankie, and the other to me. "But don't think I'm going to make a habit of running round after you! Have a good time – and I'll see you tomorrow."

"Quick," Frankie said, as her mum hurried back to the car. "We've got to get these in your freezer!"

"What are they?" I asked, puzzled.

"I'll show you when we're inside," Frankie said. "But they'll have started melting on the way over, so hurry up and open the front door!"

"It *is* open—" I began, and then I saw that it wasn't. It must have swung shut while we were talking to Frankie's mum.

We looked at each other in horror for a

second, and then I remembered. "It's all right," I said. "Molly's in."

I put the box down and rang the doorbell like crazy. Nothing happened at first, so I rang even harder and started hammering on the door.

At last Molly heard me, but she didn't come to the door. She opened the window upstairs and leant out.

"Who is it?" she called, sounding very nervous. "Why are you making so much noise? My dad's here! He's very angry!"

I stood back so she could see me. "Molly! It's me! Open the door! And hurry up about it!"

I can't believe Molly sometimes. She is *so* mean. Of course any normal, decent person would have come and opened the door if they saw their sister stuck outside. But, as you know, Molly isn't a normal, decent person and she didn't – she just stared at me.

"What are you doing out there?" she asked.

"Just open the door!" I yelled.

Frankie was peering into the box she was holding, looking anxious. A trickle of something red was creeping out of the bottom.

"I'm busy," Molly said, and would you believe it? She slammed the window shut and disappeared.

I jammed my finger on the doorbell so it sounded like a fire alarm – but it didn't make any difference. My horrible ghastly monster sister just ignored it.

"Can't we get in through the back door?" Frankie asked.

We rushed round the side of the house, but the back door was firmly locked. We tried every window, and I even attempted climbing up a drainpipe – but it was useless. Our house was like a super-safe prison – and we were on the outside.

I shook my head gloomily, as we walked back round to the front. "It's no good," I said. "It's because of all the burglaries. Before Dad went out he told me and Mum to keep everything triple locked. And I know all the downstairs windows are shut because I locked them myself."

"Fantastic," said Frankie, and she sat down on the front step. I gave the doorbell one last punch. It gave a weird clunk, and stopped ringing. When I tried again, nothing happened.

"Well, that's blown it," I said, and sat on the step beside Frankie. The trickle of red from the box was longer now. It looked exactly like blood, and I stared at it.

"Frankie – what exactly is in these boxes?"

Frankie sighed heavily. "It was the best thing ever. Look!" And she opened the first box. Inside was something that looked exactly like a head with pale green sightless eyes gazing up at me. Well, it was almost like a head, but a head that was getting softer and squishier by the second.

"Wow!" I gasped. "Sculpted ice cream. It's utterly *awesome*!"

"It was," Frankie said. "I spent hours on it. The eyes are grapes, by the way... they're probably all that'll be left soon."

"What's in the other box?" I asked, and she opened the lid. Inside was a plate with a melting block of – frozen blood?

"It's beetroot and raspberries mashed up," Frankie said, and she sounded even more gloomy. "I was going to mash it some more and put the head on it… but it's ruined now."

"I'll kill Molly," I said.

"Maybe we could put *her* head on the plate," Frankie said, but at that moment it didn't sound much like a joke.

Suddenly I sat up. I'd thought of something to make us feel more cheerful. "Hey," I said, "Molly's going to be in *mega* trouble with Mum for shutting us out! It's all Molly's fault that this has happened."

"Yeah," Frankie agreed, and we both felt a tiny bit better.

We sat on the step for at least ten minutes watching Frankie's ice-cream head gradually dissolve. Actually, after two minutes we gave in and ate some of it. After all, we couldn't let it go to waste, could we? But it wasn't long before it was just a soggy mess with the two grapes swimming in the middle.

"Do you think we'd better move the other box?" Frankie asked. "It seems to have made a bit of a mess."

I looked across, and she was right. The blood mixture was dripping all the way down the steps. "Hmm," I said. "It's a pity we can't leave it like that. It'd be a great entrance for the others – blood on the doorstep!"

Frankie laughed, but we both knew my mum wouldn't agree with us. Mums are so boring when it comes to things like blood.

"Hey, Frankie!" I leapt to my feet. I'd suddenly had an amazing flash of inspiration. "We could still use it! We could make a trail of blood drops!"

Frankie's eyes shone. "Wicked! *A trail of gruesome spots leads the detectives in and out of the bushes and trees. In and out they hurried, until they found—*"

"A body!" We both yelled together, and then we collapsed, laughing.

We did a fantastic job – we made the most life-like trail of blood you ever saw. It started just round the corner of the house, because I didn't want Mum telling us to wash it away before we'd shown Rosie, Lyndz and Fliss. We started with a few drops, and then a few more – and then a big puddle. Actually, we didn't mean to make it quite so big but the plate slipped.

Frankie said it didn't matter. "We can pretend that's where the victim tried to pull the knife out of his back," she said.

It looked wonderfully ghoulish.

We put a few more drops on the bushes, but there wasn't much mixture left to do anything else.

"We ought to make a body, and half-hide it under the bushes," I said.

Frankie nodded. "Or we could just leave half a body!"

You can see why Frankie's my very best

friend. She likes blood and gore as much as I do!

After we'd finished the blood trail we took both boxes round the back of the house and dumped them in the bin. Quite a lot of the melted ice cream dribbled out on the way, but there wasn't anything we could do about it. We couldn't get back into the house to fetch any buckets of water or anything like that. If anyone said anything, it was all Molly's fault.

As we wandered back to the front door Mum came walking up the path with some strange woman beside her – our new neighbour!

"This is our house," Mum was saying. "It's—" And then she saw us. Her jaw did the thunking open thing mine's been doing for days, but the woman screamed. She really did! And she clutched at my mum!

Mum is made of steel. She put her jaw back in place, and glared at me. "Is this your idea of a Friday 13th joke?" she began. "Just *look* at the state you're both in!"

She was right. Frankie and I did look rather gruesome. I suppose the beetroot mixture had got all over us while we were laying our trail.

"Mum," I said. "Mum, it really and truly isn't our fault – we got locked out and Molly wouldn't let us back in!"

By the time we'd finished explaining what had happened, Mum was steaming mad with Molly, just as we'd hoped.

"That's it!" she said. "There's no way that young lady's going out tonight. She's grounded!"

Frankie and I gasped. That wasn't part of the plan. Mum couldn't do that – not *tonight*!

But she did. Even though I begged her not to. Even though Frankie begged her not to. We pleaded. We said it was all our fault. But it was no use. The new neighbour didn't help, either. She kept going on about how dangerous it was, us two little girlies being outside with a manic burglar tramping round the area. That made up Mum's mind. Molly was not going anywhere that night.

Frankie and I made faces at each other as we tipped soapy water over the front steps.

"If only the door hadn't shut," I said. "That was so unlucky."

Frankie nodded. "Friday 13th," she said. "Bad luck day!"

And it was only just beginning…

CHAPTER SIX

Mum realised how unfair it was that Molly being grounded had ruined our plans for the sleepover, so to make it up to us she said we could have the sleepover in Emma's room – as long as we *promised to be careful and not spoil anything*.

But thanks to Molly the Monster we were only just getting ready to make our scary noises tape when Rosie arrived. We didn't hear her, of course, because of the doorbell not working and Emma's room being at the back of the house, so Molly came and told us Rosie had arrived. No, she wasn't being nice to us. She was just being a creep because Mum had been so angry with her.

We both charged past Molly and rushed downstairs to see Rosie. Her bowl of spaghetti was super mega gross! It was a sort of horrible grey colour, and the currants looked exactly like dead flies... or even worse! We shoved it in the fridge, and dragged Rosie upstairs to help with the tape.

Emma has this totally fabulous stereo with a proper microphone and two tape decks, so we made one tape and then added more and more horrible noises on top. And we weren't spoiling anything that belonged to Emma: I was using all my own tapes. We were just borrowing her equipment.

Rosie whispered into the microphone, and Frankie did her best ever ghostly wails. I squeaked the door and moaned and groaned. Then we discovered that if we went a bit further away we could make it sound more echoey, so we opened the door and Rosie and I went down the stairs to make hollow footsteps.

Frankie waited until we were in position, and then switched on the microphone. As we stamped up the stairs she stamped down, making the most creepy ghastly chuckles. We were really enjoying ourselves, and Rosie was doing one final hideous cackle when—

Bang! Molly came storming out of her room.

"Can't you kids *shut up*?" she screeched. "You don't need to play your silly games on the stairs! It's bad enough having you shrieking and yelling in poor Emma's room!"

Of course the microphone recorded it all. We didn't bother answering her – we flew back to turn the microphone off, and then we slammed Emma's door.

"Doom and Disaster!" I said.

"Let's play it back," Frankie suggested. "Maybe Molly sounds like a hideous awful witch."

Rosie and I giggled, and we rewound the tape and pressed Play.

It was the most fantastical ghoulish tape ever – until Molly came on. She did sound dreadful. But not much like a witch.

"Shall we tape over it?" Rosie asked.

"No – let's leave it!" I said. "We'll tell Lyndz and Fliss we've got the only recording ever made of a horrible monster!"

We were in the kitchen making the green slime when Fliss and Lyndz arrived. Fliss knocked so politely we didn't hear her, but Lyndz gave the letter box a real hammering.

"Great!" I said when we were all in the kitchen. "The Sleepover Club's in action again! And we've got some real surprises for you... especially in the garden!"

Fliss was looking anxious already. She kept peering over her shoulder and jumping at the slightest noise, and now she gave a little squeak. "My mum says we're all to stay indoors," she said. "She says you don't know who might be watching the house to see if it's a good moment to get in."

I caught Frankie's eye, and we both burst

out laughing.

Fliss went very pink. "It's nothing to laugh about," she said.

"No," I said, "it's not that – we're laughing because Frankie and I spent *hours* outside today trying to get in and we couldn't! This house has to be the most burglar-proof house in the whole world!"

"Oh," Fliss said, and she began to look a bit better.

Then Frankie and I told the others about how Molly had refused to let us in and how Frankie's ice-cream head had been ruined.

When they'd heard the whole story, that settled it. We all made a vow of terrible revenge.

"We could haunt her all night," Frankie suggested.

"How about making her an apple-pie bed?" Lyndz giggled.

"Maybe we could tap on her window!" Rosie said.

Fliss went twitchy again. "But then we'd have to go outside!"

"Don't worry, we'll think of something! " I said, then I decided to change the subject. "Can we see your cake, Fliss?"

"Oh, yes! It's the best!" Fliss hurried out to the hall, and came back with a cake tin.

For once Fliss wasn't exaggerating. The cake *was* mega brilliant! It had two sorts of green swirled together, and there were jelly worms popping out of the icing and jelly spiders crouching round the bottom. We all ooohed and aaahed, and told Fliss how clever she was. Fliss smiled from ear to ear.

"I had some jelly worms left over," she said. "Here – I thought they might be useful."

"Great! We can put them in the slime," I said. "Where's your pizza, Lyndz?"

Lyndz grinned. "Wait and see!" she said.

"That's not fair!" Rosie said. "We've seen Fliss's cake!"

Lyndz just went on grinning and shook her head.

We couldn't hassle her any more because just then Mum came into the kitchen. "Are you lot still in here?" she said. "I need to get something ready for Dad – he's rushing in before his meeting—" She stopped when she saw the cake. "Goodness! That *is* clever!" Fliss blushed, and looked really pleased with herself again.

"It's nothing," she said in the sort of voice that means "Yes, I am very clever and I know I am!"

"It's OK, Mum," I said. "All we've got to do is bung the slime in the fridge and then we'll go upstairs."

"Fine," Mum said. "But don't forget—"

"Not to spoil anything of Emma's!" I finished her sentence for her.

We finished our stuff in the kitchen and galloped up the stairs to Emma's room.

"Come on," I said, "let's make ourselves some space here. Emma's away all weekend, so she'll never know. We can put everything back tomorrow."

"Isn't that spoiling things?" Fliss asked.

"No," I said. "It's *moving* things. If we move everything against the wall we can really spread out tonight. The way it is now we couldn't swing a cat."

Fliss giggled. "Poor cat!"

"I can swing a teddy!" Frankie said, and she whirled Emma's white bear round her head.

Crash! Emma's bedside lamp leapt off the table, and Rosie, Lyndz, Fliss and I cackled with laughter.

"Ooops!" Frankie got down on her hands and knees and picked it up again. "Maybe you were right, Kenny! There isn't any room to swing anything!"

We heaved and shoved and pushed the furniture right up against the walls, and piled Emma's clothes and shoes on one of the beds. Then we looked round.

"Wow!" Lyndz was dead impressed. "There's room to swing dozens of cats in here now!"

"Whoopee!" Frankie grabbed the white teddy again and swung it madly round her head. "Room to swing a teddy!"

Lyndz snatched up a green frog, and Rosie and Fliss fought over a fluffy bunny.

Fliss won, so Rosie pounced on a pink giraffe. I found a squashy elephant… and we swung them all round and round and round!

"Room to swing a jungle!" I yelled, and I let the elephant fly… and the elephant hit Rosie, and Rosie fell over onto Fliss, and Fliss whacked Lyndz with her fluffy bunny and Lyndz sent her green frog zooming across the room and—

Crash! The bedside lamp went flying for a second time.

This time the lamp broke. Seriously broke. Doom! The bottom bit was made of pink china (it was typical of Emma to have everything in prissy pink!) and the pink china was now in bits. The shade was bent too.

We went rather quiet for a moment as we looked at the wreckage.

"Sorry," Lyndz said.

"We're all to blame," Frankie said, and I nodded.

"If it's anyone's fault it's the frog's," Rosie said, and Frankie giggled. "Ground that frog!"

"Stop its pocket money!" I said.

"We could try and mend it," Fliss said. She was picking up the pieces. "Have you got any of that Super Glue stuff?"

"I don't know," I said. "There might be some in the kitchen. But Emma's bound to notice."

"Let's try anyway," Lyndz said.

"Mum'll still be cooking," I said. "We can go and look for the glue later. Anyway, there's no hurry. Emma's not back until Sunday night."

Down in the hall the telephone began to ring. Someone – or some*thing*! – must have heard what I'd just said, because two minutes later Molly came thundering up the stairs and stuck her head round the door. "Emma's got to come home tonight," she said with a great big silly grin on her face. "Jade's house has been burgled, and Emma can't stay after all!"

Molly looked round Emma's room at all the piled up furniture. "Ha! Looks like *you'll* be in big trouble now!" And she flounced out.

Emma coming home? We stared at each other.

Fliss put on her drama queen face. "I knew it!" she said, and she waved her arms. "It's because it's Friday 13th! Everything's bound to go wrong!"

CHAPTER SEVEN

"I'm going to ask Mum if it's true," I said, once I'd got over the shock. "The monster might have made it up – it's just the low-down kind of trick she likes to play."

As it turned out it *was* true – but it wasn't quite as bad as Molly had made it sound. Emma couldn't stay the night, but she and Jade had gone out to have a pizza, and Dad was going to collect her on the way back from his meeting.

"It's going to be quite late, so Emma may as well sleep in your room with Molly tonight," Mum said.

Sleepover on Friday 13th

I heaved a huge sigh of relief – inside. Outside I just nodded. "OK," I said.

Mum gave me a suspicious sort of look. "I hope you haven't been making a mess up there," she said. "Molly says you've been moving furniture."

"We only moved things a little," I said. "And we do that in my room."

"Fine." Mum went on stirring something in a saucepan. "Molly and I are eating with Dad, so you lot can do your feasting on green cake afterwards in peace."

"Thanks, Mum, you're the best," I said, and gave her a hug.

I was going back up the stairs when I heard Dad coming in. I gave a quick wave over the banisters, and then shot back into Emma's room to tell the others not to panic – yet!

"We can sort the room out in the morning," I said.

Fliss was peering out of the window. "I'm sure I heard a strange noise," she said. "Do you think there's someone down there?" She was looking twitchy again.

"I expect it's Dad," I said. "He's just come home."

"Oh," Fliss said, but she didn't sound very convinced.

"Let's go and see!" Frankie said, and she made a face at me behind Fliss's back, and mouthed, "*Blood trail*!"

"Oh no!" Fliss squeaked. "We ought to stay inside!"

"It'll be OK with all of us," Lyndz said, and she grinned. "What burglar would take on the Sleepover Club?"

Even Fliss smiled a little. "I still don't think we shou—" she began, but she didn't sound so certain.

"Come on!" Lyndz grabbed her hand. "We can make sure it's all clear down there while it's still light! We'll check out the bushes!"

"Only a mini burglar could hide in your garden," Rosie said.

"That's it!" I said. "The burglar's only sixty centimetres tall – and that's why no one's found him yet!"

Sleepover on Friday 13th

We were halfway down the stairs when Frankie suddenly stopped. "Sssh!" she said. "We sound like a herd of elephants! From now on we've got to go on tiptoe!"

"Tippytoe! Tippytoe! Hunting burglars! Here we go!" giggled Lyndz, and we got in a line and tiptoed down the rest of the stairs and out of the front door. (We made sure we left it on the latch this time. Frankie and I weren't taking any more chances!)

It was beginning to get dark as we crept round the side of the house. Frankie was in front, then me, then Lyndz, then Rosie, and then Fliss.

"Tippytoe! Tippytoe! Tippytoe!" sang Lyndz, and we all tiptoed in time down the path, until—

"Look!" Frankie did her mega-thrill, over-the-top acting voice and stopped dead on the path.

We all crashed into each other, and somehow Fliss ended up at the front – so she saw the trail of blood before Lyndz or Rosie. And she screamed...

I think the rest of us were as frightened by Fliss's scream as she was frightened by the blood. I know my heart gave a huge walloping leap inside my chest, and I heard Lyndz gasp beside me. When someone really truly screams for real, it's not a nice noise at all – it's *really* scary! And then Fliss turned and she *ran* back into the house, and of course we all tore after her.

If it had been me I think I'd have headed straight for the grown-ups, but Fliss didn't – luckily for us. She zoomed up to Emma's room, and when we got there she was shaking all over and trying to stuff her pyjamas into her bag.

"Fliss, what are you doing?" I asked.

She looked up, and her face was a horrible colour – completely grey-green. "I want to go home," she said. "I saw blood all over your path! I want my mum! I'm scared!"

I looked at Frankie, and Frankie looked at me. "I'm really sorry, Fliss," I said. "It wasn't blood – it was just raspberry juice from Frankie's pudding."

"It melted when we were shut outside," Frankie said. "And it seemed a pity to waste it all – so we trailed it round the path."

"Are you sure it wasn't blood?" Fliss still looked like a frightened rabbit, but at least she'd stopped shaking. She'd stopped trying to pack her pyjamas, too.

I suddenly remembered what Dad had told me about people who'd had a terrible fright. You should keep them warm, and if there's no chance of them having any kind of internal injury, you should give them a warm drink.

"Hang on!" I said. "Frankie, put my duvet round Fliss!" and I rushed off downstairs.

Molly and Mum were just finishing eating, and Dad had made a pot of tea. Just the thing!

"Can I take a cup of tea up to Fliss?" I said. "She's – she's a bit cold."

"I thought I heard you go outside," Mum said. "Don't go out again, though – it's getting dark now."

I wondered why they hadn't heard Fliss

scream. The noise was still ringing inside my head. Probably Molly had been bleating on about some boring thing she was doing at school – or maybe they thought it was on the TV. I could hear it mumbling away in the sitting room.

I poured out the tea, shoved in a big spoonful of sugar, and got out of the door as fast as I could before anyone asked me any awkward questions.

Upstairs, Fliss was much better. She was wrapped up in my duvet, and Lyndz was fussing round her in just the way Fliss likes best. She drank the tea, and her face went back to its normal colour.

"It's a good thing we didn't have time to make a body!" Frankie said cheerfully. "Fliss would have had a hundred fits then!"

"Mum says I'm very sensitive," Fliss said, sounding really pleased about it. Then she shivered again. "The blood did look real, though!"

"I never got a chance to see it properly," Rosie said in a disappointed voice, and that made us all laugh.

There was a knock on the door. "Kitchen's clear!" Dad said, and we heard him stomping off into my parent's room. I guessed he was going to get ready for his meeting.

"I say it's food time!" shouted Lyndz. "Can I go down and put my pizza in the oven first? You lot stay up here for two minutes – I don't want anyone seeing it until it's ready!"

We counted one hundred and twenty hippopotamuses to give Lyndz time to sort out her pizza, and then we couldn't wait any longer. We rushed downstairs to sort out our ghoulish grub. Fliss still seemed to be suffering from shock, and she jumped a mile when Rosie dropped a spoon. I wished she'd get back to normal soon. I was feeling a little guilty that we'd scared her half to death!

When Lyndz finally pulled the pizza out of the oven we all gasped again. Usually Frankie is the one who makes pizzas – her dad is famous for them – and Lyndz's pizza wasn't fab in the way Frankie's are. But it *was* fabulously gross. For a start it was green – a muddy, been buried for ages sort of green. It was folded over in half, so the two edges looked a bit like horrible ghoulish lips... and there were fingers sticking out! Horrible, drooping, floppy, *shiny pink* fingers, with oozy blood dribbling out between each of them. (Actually they were sausages, but they really looked like fingers.)

We all shouted *yuck*! together – it was *so* brilliant!

We carried all the food upstairs; during sleepovers, we always eat our food in the bedroom – it's much more fun. The green slime wibbled and wobbled like mad; I'd filled the bowl rather full, but we just about managed not to spill it. At least, not much of it – a little slimed its way out when Rosie tried to open the door with one hand and hold the bowl with the other. It looked as if a large slug had been trying to ooze its way into Emma's room!

We put the food on the floor, snuggled into our sleeping bags and turned the lights off. Then we pulled out our torches. Have

you ever eaten like that? It's awesome!
Although you don't always see when things
get spilt.

"Let's put our horror tape on!" Frankie
suggested.

"Great idea," I said.

We had to put the light back on to see
what we were doing with the stereo, but we
turned it off again after I'd pressed Play.

The tape had only been on for a second
when Fliss jumped up. "I want the light back
on," she said, scrambling through all the
food to the light switch. Then she turned
the tape off. "It's HORRIBLE!" she said,
shivering.

Sometimes I think Fliss is the biggest
wimp I've ever met. We tried everything we
could think of, but there was no way we
could persuade her to let us put the tape on
in the dark. She said she didn't mind the
torches, but no tape. If we wanted the tape
she wanted the light on. In the end we gave
in. We didn't play the tape.

The food was some of the best ever.

Rosie's grey spaghetti was kind of chewy, but it didn't matter. Lyndz said it was a bowl of horror worms and we could only eat them by sucking them up! We took it in turn slurping them out of the bowl and we slurped the slime as well. It was wicked! The pizza didn't just look awesome, it tasted scrummy, too. We'd saved the cake for the very last. Fliss began to smile a lot more when we got near the time to cut the cake!

"We should each cut a slice and wish," she said. "Then maybe we won't have any more bad luck."

We all agreed that was a great idea, and I handed Fliss the knife. "You go first," I said, and Fliss held it over the green jelly-worm icing.

"I wish—" she began, but didn't get any further.

"Laura! I want you and all your friends down here *at once!*"

It was Dad. He was shouting up the stairs, and he sounded *mad*.

CHAPTER EIGHT

We went out to the hall, and there was Dad. At least, it had to be Dad because the thing standing there had Dad's voice and it was Dad's height – but otherwise you couldn't really tell because it was snow white. Or rather flour white… and I knew it was flour because he was holding the cat hot-water bottle in his hand. He looked incredibly weird – I mean, I knew it was my Dad, but he looked like a ghost!

The others didn't know what to think. Fliss stared with her eyes out on stalks. Rosie and Frankie and Lyndz began to giggle

– but they soon stopped when they saw my dad's face. If this was a ghost, it was a very, very *angry* ghost!

Oooooops! I couldn't help thinking that we were having enough bad luck to last us for years and years...

"Is this one of your ridiculous Friday 13th tricks?" Dad roared. "I was in the kitchen, just about to go to a *very* important meeting – and *whoomp*! I get attacked by a flying hot-water bottle. One minute I'm standing minding my own business and finishing a quiet cup of tea, and the next – *furry cats come zooming out of cupboards*. And my best suit is ruined!"

I opened my mouth to say it was all my fault, and none of the others knew about it – but I never got the chance. Just then Mum came out of the sitting room – she saw Dad and she began to laugh. Actually laugh!

"I'm sorry," she said, "but you do look funny. Whatever happened?"

Dad tried to look dignified, but it wasn't easy. He waved the furry hot-water bottle in the air. "It's one of Laura's silly tricks!" he said. "Or one of her friend's! They're all as bad as each other! I was looking for the shoe polish and this" – he waved the cat again – "flew out of the top cupboard in the kitchen and covered me with some kind of white dust!"

I opened my mouth again, but Mum got in there first.

"Oh no!" she said, and she began to dust Dad down. "Do you know, I think for once Kenny's not to blame? I think it's *my* fault! I put that cat away ages ago. I don't think Kenny even knew where it was – did you?" And Mum turned to me.

Well – what would you have done? Would you have leapt forward and said "No, it was me! I did it!"? I did dither for a milli-second. Then I said, "I didn't know it was there until today." Which *was* true… and I was thinking I'd got away with it when Mum suddenly stopped brushing.

"Just a moment," she said. "This isn't dust. It's flour – I'm sure it is!" Both she and

Dad swivelled round to look at me. I could feel myself going pink. Time to own up....

"It jumped out at me this morning," I said. "I was looking in the kitchen cupboard and it did exactly the same thing to me. It scared me off my stool!"

"So you thought you'd put it back," Mum said. "And give it a little extra dusting... so when it jumped out again it would be even better!"

Sometimes I think Mum is a mind-reader. I nodded.

"*Humph*," Mum said, and she looked at Dad. She still had a twinkle in her eye, but Dad didn't. Not at all. He was grumbling away like a volcano – I hoped he wasn't going to explode *too* loudly.

"It's all very well playing silly games," he said. "But my suit's filthy, and I'm going to be late if I don't hurry. I think we'd better talk about this tomorrow, Laura."

"Sorry, Dad," I said, and he stomped off into the kitchen.

Mum must have been able to brush the

worst of the flour off because I heard the car leave about two minutes later.

The others and I hurried back to our interrupted cake. As soon as we'd shut the door it struck me how funny Dad had looked, and I began to giggle. The others started, too, and when I told them how the furry hot-water bottle had scared me silly before breakfast they laughed even more.

"Your Dad looked like a real ghost!" Lyndz chortled, and she rolled over and over on the floor.

"We should have asked him up to eat horror worms with us!" Rosie cackled. "Whooo! Whoooo! Whooooo! All the worms would have run away!"

"If he walked round the streets like that he'd scare the burglar into the middle of next week!" hooted Frankie.

"I'm glad that furry thing didn't jump out when we were in the kitchen," Fliss said. "I think I'd have died of fright!" She probably would have, too, knowing Fliss!

We sat down again to cut the cake, but we

were all really giggly. You know what it's like when anything at all makes you laugh, even if it's not really funny? Well, we were like that – even Fliss. We waved jelly worms at each other, and we made the jelly spiders plop into the remains of the green slime… and we began to tell ghost stories. We sat in the dark and made them up as we went along, and our ideas became more and more ridiculous.

Lyndz started off the story; she said she'd heard that there was a headless woman who walked round and round the house at midnight where a Dreadful Deed had been done.

Then Rosie said that it must be a house near where she lived, because there were often strange wailings and howlings in the night. She said there were two dogs who howled, but they didn't sound like dogs at all.

Frankie went next and said that in the old days people believed evil spirits could change into dogs, and this was what these dogs were. We took it in turns to describe what they looked like – "glowing red eyes!" and "slobbering jaws!" and "huge, ginormous teeth!"

"And then," Frankie said, and she made her voice go very deep and scary, "one of the monster dogs began creeping and crawling along the road… and it saw—"

"Molly the Monster!" I interrupted. "And both dogs turned round and ran away as fast as they could go!" And we all burst into giggles all over again.

"We still haven't played that tape," I said at last. "Fliss, if we put the light on can we play it? Only I must warn you, there's a real live monster at the end!"

Fliss pulled a long face and looked as if she was about to say no again, but we all pleaded with her until she had to give in.

"All right," she said reluctantly. "As long as the light's on."

I squirmed out of my sleeping bag and began crawling across the floor to the light switch. Of course I had to climb over everyone else – and there was some furious wriggling as I wormed my way across the floor.

"I'm a *horror* worm!" I hissed. "And I'm coming to get you!"

The sleeping-bag worms wriggled this way and that as I pounced. I found knobbly worms and squashy worms and…

Yuck! I put my hand right in the slimiest squishiest thing I'd ever felt. I didn't have time to say anything, though, because a sleeping-bag worm grabbed me by the ankles and pulled me back along the floor… and the slimy stuff came with me. I tried to grab something, and there was a muffled shriek as my horrible slimy hand met Rosie's face.

Two screams in one night! Luckily Rosie doesn't scream as loudly as Fliss – and she had a mouthful of slime as well. But it was still mega-creepy.

Fliss and Lyndz and Frankie sat bolt upright, and Fliss said, "What's happening?" in a quivery voice.

"Everyone be quiet," I said. "You'll get my mum up here."

I found the light switch and turned it on.

Rosie had green slime on her face, and I had it all over my hand. The carpet had a green smear all along where I'd been dragged – but at least we knew it was only jelly. It hadn't felt like jelly when I put my hand in it, though; I suppose that's what happens when you're in the dark.

I took Rosie to the bathroom to clean herself up, and while I was there I grabbed a towel. The carpet looked better after we'd rubbed it a bit.

"It's only wet," Frankie said. "After all, that's all jelly slime is – mostly water. It'll have dried by the morning."

Just to be on the safe side we moved the rest of the food onto one of the beds out of our way.

"Did you see the moonlight when we were in the bathroom?" Rosie asked as we climbed back into our sleeping bags. "We ought to open the curtains. It's really bright!"

"What about the tape?" Fliss asked.

"I'll put it on in a minute," I said. "Let's look at the moonlight first."

We opened the curtains and turned the light off. Rosie was quite right. The moon *was* very bright – it was almost like having the light on.

"Open the window," Frankie said. "You can see everything out there!"

We opened the window, and peered out. It was very quiet outside, and the moonlight made long shadows across the path.

"It looks magical!" Fliss said, wistfully.

We were quite quiet for a moment or two while we looked outside. And then we saw it. Something – someone – was climbing very carefully over the fence. The fence into *my garden*.

CHAPTER NINE

You'd have thought one of us would have screamed – especially Fliss. But we didn't. It was very strange. Somehow the idea of a burglar was much *much* more scary than the real thing. Or perhaps it was because we were safely inside a big house with lots of locks on all the doors, and Mum was downstairs. The burglar looked quite small and skinny, too – not at all massive and thuggish.

"Is it really a burglar?" Rosie whispered.

"I think so," I whispered back.

The burglar rubbed his hands on his

trousers as he came away from the fence. We saw him look at the house – *my house*! and then move very softly through the plants and bushes towards the path. It was like watching a cat, or some other night animal.

"We ought to tell Mum," I whispered, but I didn't get up. After all, he hadn't done anything yet. He was just walking towards the path…

Yowl! Eeeeeeeeeeeeeeeeeek! Owwwwwwwllll llllllllllllie Wowlie!

It was our horror tape, and it was playing at the sort of volume that cracks your ears open and splits your head. I leapt a million miles in the air – but that was nothing to the way the burglar jumped. He jumped as if someone had given him a zillion megawatt electric shock, spun round – and fell flat on his back with a massive *thwack*!

We were frozen rigid. We hung out of the window staring.

"Is he dead?" Frankie whispered.

"I'd better get Mum!" I said, and hurtled

off down the stairs.

Mum was halfway up the stairs, anyway. I guess she couldn't have missed the noise – which was still blaring out. She could see at once that something was up, though – and when I blurted out, "Mum! Mum! There's a burglar dead on the path!" she flew to the phone.

Have you ever had to dial 999? I've always wanted to – and now Mum was doing it! She was really calm and cool as well. I'd have probably forgotten my address, my telephone number *and* my name!

"Right," Mum said as she snapped down the receiver. "Where's this burglar?"

"You mustn't go outside!" I gasped. "Supposing he was only winded? He might hurt us!"

"I wasn't going to," Mum said. "We'll look out of the window."

Our tape suddenly went quiet. Frankie came to the top of the stairs. "He's still there!" she whispered down. "He's moved a little – but he hasn't got up!"

Molly burst into the hall. "What's going on?" she said. She glared at me. "More of your silly baby Friday 13th games, I suppose."

"Molly," Mum said, "just go back into the sitting room. There's nothing to worry about."

I was so proud of my mum! She was still dead calm. Ferocious burglars were lurking in our garden, and she was acting as cool as a cucumber!

Molly gave me a furious look and disappeared.

When we looked out of the dining-room window I could see the burglar much better. He really did look small.

"He's not wearing a mask," I said.

"No," Mum said. "And he's not wearing a black-and-white striped top or carrying a bag on his back marked SWAG, either!

The burglar started to move. He tried to sit up, but there seemed to be something wrong with his leg.

"Dear me," Mum said suddenly. "He must

be badly hurt! Look! He's sitting in a pool of blood! Poor man! I'd better go and see if I can help him!"

"Oh!" I said, and a massive flash of understanding zoomed into my brain. I knew why the burglar had fallen over. He'd slipped – in our trail.

"Hang on, Mum!" I said. "It isn't *real* blood. It's the melted stuff from Frankie's pudding. Rather a lot of it got – er – spilt on the path. That's why he slipped!"

I think Mum was about to say something when we heard the police cars.

DEE – DAW – DEE – DAW – DEE – DAW

I've heard them hundreds of times before, but this time was different. This time they were coming to *our* house! The burglar heard it, too, and he tried to get up again – but he couldn't.

Mum went to the front door. "Laura," she said, "go back upstairs."

"But Mum—" I protested.

"Go!" Mum said, and when she talks in that tone of voice I do as I'm told. Fast!

Rosie, Lyndz, Frankie and Fliss grabbed me as I came through the door. They all started speaking at once.

"We heard the police car!"

"Look – he's trying to move!"

"Here they come! I can see the lights!"

"Why did he fall over? Is he all right?"

And then four policemen came charging into our garden with the biggest torches you ever saw – and one of them was kneeling by the burglar checking to see where he was hurt.

"There's a lot of blood around here, Sarge," a big policeman said. "Where d'you think it's come from?"

Another policeman bent down and peered with his torch at the path. Frankie and I held our breath. Our trail of blood glistened very red in the beam of light. Then the policeman stood up, and we could see him grinning. His teeth flashed in the moonlight. "That's not blood, Sarge. It's jam – or something very like it!"

"What's going on? Is anyone hurt? I'm a

doctor!" It was Dad, hurrying to the scene of the crime. The whole thing was exactly like something on TV! And we were up at our window watching it for real!

"Well, sir – if you'd be kind enough to look at this young fellow," a policeman said.

We could see Dad checking the burglar by the light of the police torches.

"Hmm," said Dad. "Broken ankle, I'd say. You'd be best off getting him to a hospital for an X-ray." Then he suddenly leant forward, and peered at the burglar. "Hang on a moment. I know you! You were hanging around my surgery last week! And I saw you trying the car doors in the car park!"

The sergeant looked excited. "Could you swear to that, sir?"

"I certainly could," Dad said. "But what's going on? What are you all doing in my garden?"

I was dying to yell out that it was the burglar, and that we'd caught him – but I didn't. Mum was out there now as well, and I thought it might be best if she explained things. I went on watching with the others.

At least, we went on watching for another minute, and then the light switched on behind us – and there was Emma.

No burglar could ever be as terrifying as Emma in a really furious mood – and this time she wasn't just really furious. She was mega mega *mega* furious. She shouted and yelled and screamed at us, and called us all sorts of names. Molly couldn't resist joining in, and every time Emma slowed down Molly would point out some other thing that we'd done – like the slimy wet patch on the carpet, or the broken lamp, or the cake crumbs everywhere, or the tape in her stereo.

We didn't say anything. Emma wouldn't have listened if we had.

GOODBYE

Mum and Dad finally waved the police goodbye, and came back in. The burglar went off with the police in their car.

As soon as Mum was in earshot Emma started shrieking at her. "Come and look!" she yelled. "Come and see what they've done to my room! She *knows* she's not allowed in here – and all her horrible little friends are here, too, and they've *wrecked* my room!"

Molly just stood there and sniggered.

Dad and Mum appeared in the doorway, and Dad put his arm round Emma's shoulders – but he gave us a huge wink.

"They'll clear it all up in the morning," he said. "I know they get daft ideas in their heads – and some are dafter than others – but tonight's a little bit different. You see, your sister and her friends have caught a burglar!" And he gently shooed Emma and Molly away.

Well you'd think that we'd have got some kind of medal for catching a burglar, wouldn't you? Or a reward. In all the books you read there are always huge rewards. But us? We ended up spending the next morning cleaning up Emma's room!

We did get our picture in *The Mercury* though. A reporter came and took our photo all together, grinning like monkeys. He asked us if we often played at catching burglars and loads of other questions. Then of course we all got really excited about how we were going to become local celebrities, given special treatment wherever we went and generally made a fuss of, but when the paper came out it sounded as if we were about six. Emma and Molly teased me about it for ages.

Yes, Emma is finally speaking to me again. She even apologised for calling the others horrible! She's OK really. She doesn't hold grudges, unlike Molly. Mind you I do have to buy her a new lamp and pay to have the carpet cleaned. Mum's taking the money out of my allowance – she said it was only fair.

We had to scrub the garden path, too. I thought the police might want to see all the footprints going up and down, but as Dad said, what was the point? They'd caught the burglar. So – it was soapy water and scrubbing brushes for the Sleepover Club. Actually, we had quite a lot of fun. It got very bubbly…

And at least we weren't grounded, so we can have another sleepover really soon – I'll look forward to seeing you there. I've got a feeling it may not be as eventful as Friday 13th was – but with the Sleepover Club you never can tell!

P.S. Just in case you were wondering, I've

come back to tell you. Or maybe you've already guessed who switched on the tape – and gave the burglar the fright of his life? I didn't. I couldn't believe it when Frankie told me. It was Fliss! There may be some hope for her after all…

See ya!